i haiku you

betsy snyder

random house 🏠 new york

this book is especially for:

your everyday song,
my favorite alarm clock—
good morning to you!

hey there, snow angel,
we make perfect valentines—
match made in heaven

noodles so yummy,
love letters for your tummy—
warm alphabet soup

your rainbow colors
come out to play when it pours—
chase the gray away

love is in the air—
every time our hearts meet up,
i get butterflies

what are the chances?

maybe one in a million?

what luck i found you!

a wheely fun ride
when your feet touch the pedals—
BEEP! BEEP! bicycle

you hug away tears,
making boo-boos all better—
best teddy ever

taste buds are cheering
for a squeeze of your sunshine—
HOORAY, lemonade!

purple popsicle,
you're the coolest summer treat—
i love every drop

little by little

i love watching you grow up,

each and every inch

achy-heartbreak love,

miss-you-so-much-it-hurts love.

please hurry home, love

it's quite clear to me
after hanging out with you—
we're friends at first sight

you be my jelly,

i'll be your peanut butter—

let's stick together!

wiggle-wag tail love,
sloppy-smoochy-poochy love,
true-furry-friend love!

toasty together—
happy-camper sandwiches,
ooey-gooey s'mores

while we are apart,

stars wink a message to you—

i (twinkle) love you

from your button nose
to your little piggy toes,
i luv-a-dub you!

shiny mister moon —

your smile keeps me company

when the lights go out

snuggles and stories—

best way to wrap up the day . . .

a

    happy

        ending

for jeffrey—
because I love you more
than purple popsicles

special thanks to my editor, heidi

Copyright © 2012 by Betsy E. Snyder

All rights reserved. Published in the United States by Random House Children's Books,
a division of Random House, Inc., New York.
Random House and the colophon are registered trademarks of Random House, Inc.

Visit us on the Web! randomhouse.com/kids
Educators and librarians, for a variety of teaching tools, visit us at RHTeachersLibrarians.com

Library of Congress Cataloging-in-Publication Data
Snyder, Betsy E.
I haiku you / Betsy Snyder. — 1st ed.
p. cm.
ISBN 978-0-375-86750-7 (trade) — ISBN 978-0-375-96750-4 (lib. bdg.) —
ISBN 978-0-375-98126-5 (ebook)
1. Haiku, American. 2. Children's poetry, American. I. Title.
PS3619.N924I25 2012
811'.6—dc23 2012008884

MANUFACTURED IN MALAYSIA
10 9 8 7 6 5 4   First Edition